The Fairy Painting

Tina—
Believe!
Stacey DuFord

Written by Stacey DuFord

Illustrated by Wendy Popko

Mackinac Island Press

First Edition

Library of Congress Cataloging-in-Publication Data

DuFord, Stacey and Popko, Wendy
The Fairy Painting
Summary: A young artist, a fairy and a wet painting are sent on a flurry of adventure together. *The Fairy Painting* explores loyalty, trust, responsibility and self-confidence as the little fairy's wings happen to get stuck in Elise's wet painting.
ISBN 0-9749145-3-3
Fiction

10 9 8 7 6 5 4 3 2 1

Printed and bound in Canada by Friesens, Altona, Manitoba

A Mackinac Island Press, Inc. publication

Elise loved to paint. As she lay on the grass in her backyard on a hot summer day, she picked a dandelion puff and blew its white silky pieces into the air. "I wish...I was a better painter," she thought, as she looked up hopefully at the painting on her easel. The sky still wasn't right, but the grass was perfect.

"Elise...lunch!" her mother called.

"What are you painting today?" asked her mother, after Elise ran into the house.

"Oh! I'm painting the edge of our yard. The sky isn't very good and I haven't started the trees yet, but it's the best grass I've ever painted!" Elise was out of breath.

"I'll have to come out later and see this grass," said her mother.

Elise peeked through the window and saw Duke, her dog, sniffing at her painting. She grabbed a handful of carrots and ran out the door yelling at Duke to get away.

As Elise got closer to her painting she thought Duke had smudged some of the grass with his nose. She closed her eyes, afraid to look…"I'll never paint grass that real again."

Elise opened her eyes slowly and saw that it wasn't smudged at all. Someone had painted a beautiful fairy…a two-and-a-half inch tall fairy… right at the top of the grass. Who had snuck into her yard and used her paints?

The grass was still wet but the fairy looked dry–and sparkly. Just as she put her finger up to touch the fairy….

"STOP!" yelped a little voice from the painting.

Elise stumbled back, tripping over Duke and falling hard onto the grass. She looked up at her painting in surprise.

"Is this your painting?" asked the fairy.

"Yes," Elise nodded.

"I was admiring the grass, it looked so real, then I got too close...and I got stuck," said the fairy.

"Can I do something to help you?" asked Elise, as she scrambled back up.

"No, my wings are stuck and I'm afraid I'll just have to wait. We grow new wings every two weeks and then our old ones fall off," the fairy explained. "Haven't you ever found fairy wings?"

Elise was too embarrassed to answer. Her friend Jill bragged that she had found some fairy wings once, but Elise did not believe her.

"Won't you get hungry?" asked Elise, holding out a carrot.

"Fairies don't eat carrots," she laughed. "We only eat four-leaf clovers. They make our wings shiny and bring us luck. That's why you see fairies flying near the ground; we're looking for four-leaf clovers. They're hard to find and I can tell you where to look," she continued in a whisper. "But it's a secret."

Elise's mom snuck up from behind. "Where's this beautiful grass you've painted, and who were you talking to, Elise?"

Elise looked down. "No one," she said.

"Well, no one sure got you excited," said her mom. "Oh, Elise! You didn't tell me about the beautiful fairy."

Elise looked down again. "She's new."

"You should bring your picture inside," said her mom, "before something gets stuck in the wet paint."

As her mother walked toward the house, the fairy told Elise, "grown-ups can't hear fairies talk."

"Really? Why?" Elise was fascinated.

"Grown-ups can't hear sounds that are too high," replied the fairy.

The fairy agreed to be in Elise's painting until her new wings grew in, and Elise promised to find four-leaf clovers for her to eat. They were much easier to find once the fairy told her where to look.

As she carried the painting to her bedroom, Elise was careful not to bump the fairy.

Elise emptied her pockets and put the four-leaf clovers into piles for the fairy's breakfast, lunch and dinner. There were also plenty for an afternoon snack.

The next morning Elise woke up, gave the fairy some four-leaf clovers and said, "I'm so glad you got stuck in my painting, but I don't even know your name!"

The fairy stopped eating. "We are not supposed to tell."

"Will you get in trouble?" Elise asked.

"Not exactly," the fairy replied.

"If you tell me, will I disappear?" Elise asked.

"No," said the fairy.

"Will you disappear?" asked Elise.

"When a fairy tells someone their name, they also give them a gift," the fairy explained, "like a special ability or talent."

Could I fly?" asked Elise.

"Some have asked for that," said the fairy. "Others have become beautiful singers or wonderful writers…and there's one boy who can now breathe underwater."

"Why would he want to do that?" asked Elise. The fairy shrugged. "He loves fish."

"Why don't you want to give me a gift?" asked Elise.

"A gift is a big responsibility. Fairies must use this power very carefully. It's hard to keep a secret like that, especially from the people you love," replied the fairy.

Elise's mom came into her room. "Elise, I have some errands to run and you are going to Jill's for the afternoon. Her mother will be here in a minute to pick you up."

When Elise got home at dinnertime she ran to her room to give the fairy some four-leaf clovers. Her painting was gone!

"Mom! Mom!" Elise called. "Where's my painting?"

"It's a surprise," said her mom.

"But I need to know where it is RIGHT now!" Elise said. She was very worried about the fairy. "You don't understand, Mom!"

"You'll just have to be patient," said her mom.
"I can't be patient!" Elise was becoming frantic.
"Don't worry, you'll see your painting in the morning," said her mom.

Elise tossed and turned all night worrying about the fairy. Morning finally came. Elise's mom opened her door. "Get dressed and come down for breakfast, Elise, and then we'll go see your painting."

Elise jumped into her clothes, ate quickly and ran outside to fill her pockets with more four-leaf clovers. Elise and her mom were off to see Elise's painting.

"Why are we stopping here?" Elise asked as they pulled up in front of the art institute.

"There is a children's art competition here," said her mom. "I entered your painting and everyone loved it. You should be very proud."

Elise jumped out of the car. "I don't want it here!" she shouted.

"The contest is over in a week," said her mom. "Then you can bring the painting home."

Elise ran into the art institute, charging ahead, with her footsteps echoing through the halls. She found the room with the children's art and ran to her painting.

"Fairy, I'm sorry!" she quickly whispered, before her mom caught up to her.

"I want to take my painting home," sobbed Elise, to her mom.

"Elise," said her mom calmly, "everyone here at the art institute says it's beautiful. You're a much better painter than you think you are."

Elise waited until her mom wandered off to look at the other paintings. Then she snuck some four-leaf clovers to the fairy.

"I can't take you home," said Elise. "And I can't come every day, it's too far."

"I'll be all right," said the fairy. "Just come visit me whenever you can."

Elise was so worried that time seemed to drag. Finally, a few days later at dinner, her dad said, "Tomorrow I'm going to see a fabulous fairy painting I've heard about. Does anyone want to go with me?"

Elise threw her hands in the air. "I do!" she cried. She was so excited she was going to see the fairy. The next morning she filled her pockets with four-leaf clovers.

Elise and her dad looked at all the paintings entered in the contest. When they got to hers, her dad said in a loud voice, "Why, this is the prettiest painting I've ever seen!" Everyone looked at them and Elise giggled. They looked around some more and then her dad told her it was time to go home.

"I just have to say goodbye to my painting," said Elise.

"Fine," said her dad. "I'll be talking to the mermaid statue by the door."

Elise giggled again, then walked over to her painting and gave the fairy some four-leaf clovers. The fairy ate very quickly.

"Were you really hungry?" asked Elise.

"A little," said the fairy. "But I'll be fine now."

"Come on, Elise," called her dad. "Time to go."

The night of the Art Institute Awards, Elise was amazed when they announced her name as the first place winner. As she was receiving her first place prize, a boy shouted, "How could she win first place for painting a sick fairy?"

Elise ran over to her painting. The fairy *was* sick. She put her hands in her pockets. There were no four-leaf clovers! Elise started to cry. She was so sad and she didn't know what to do. How could she have forgotten?

"Elise, what's wrong?" her mother asked.

"I want to take my painting home. Right now!"

"But people want to see the painting that won first place," said her dad.

"You said I could take it home when the contest was over," Elise cried.

"I think she's over-excited," said her mom.

Elise's dad talked to the judges and soon she and her painting were in the back seat of their car on their way home.

"Hang on, Fairy," whispered Elise. "We'll be home soon."

"Who are you talking to?" asked her mother.

"No one," said Elise sadly.

When they got home Elise took the painting right to her room and closed the door to feed the fairy some four-leaf clovers.

As the fairy slowly ate, Elise looked at her closely. She saw two sets of wings.

"Your new wings grew in," she said. "Why didn't you fly away?"

"Because," said the fairy, "I promised I would stay in your painting."

"I'm really sorry," said Elise, and she started to cry.

"But you're just a little girl," said the fairy. She flew off the painting and gave Elise a kiss on her cheek.

"Salty," said the fairy.

Elise wiped her eyes. "Do you have to leave now?" she asked.

"I'll come back and visit," said the fairy. "We are friends now and I'll miss you."

"I'll miss you, too," said Elise. "I'm sorry my mom put you in that contest and I couldn't bring you enough food."

"You did the best you could and it wasn't your fault. Now you need to fix your painting," said the fairy.

Elise looked at the painting with the fairy wings stuck in the green grass.

"Oh no!" she cried. "What am I going to do?"

"You'll have to paint a picture of me," said the fairy.

"But I can't," said Elise. "Everyone will know I didn't paint you before. I'm not that good."

"You're a wonderful painter," said the fairy, and with a smile she whispered her name into Elise's ear.

Elise looked up.

"You've been a loyal and dependable friend," said the fairy. "I think you're ready."

"But if you thought I was a really good painter already, why did you give me that gift?" asked Elise.

"Belief in yourself is the best gift of all," said the fairy.

Elise pulled out her paints and painted a fairy over the real fairy wings.